The Marmalade Plot

CW01073007

The Marmalade Plot
Copyright © 2013 Cate Howarth
All rights reserved.

ISBN: 1493621955
ISBN-13: 978-1493621958

For my Dad, the storyteller.

CHAPTER 1

'Barking dogs and soggy cornflakes'

Lena awoke with a jolt, her heart racing in that bumping way that feels like it wants to jump right out. She peered bleary-eyed through the darkness and groaned as her eyes focused on the LED display of her clock. It was four- thirty, which was a dreadful time to have your eyes open (or half open). She leaned over the edge of the bunk bed to see her younger brother, Sam. His body laid widthways across the bed, with his head positioned on the edge, his hair falling over the side like a mop. Lena giggled then lay back down and tried to get back to sleep. She gazed at the window, and her eyes began to close again. The curtains blew gently in the cool breeze.

What was the window open for? Lena sat up crossly. She leaned over the end of her bunk to stretch for the window. She heard next door's dog barking. Perhaps something woke it up too? It was barking like mad, 'ruff ruff' over and over. She shut the window softly.

The sound of the dog, now slightly muffled, progressed from incredibly annoying to soothingly repetitive as Lena began to drift off to sleep once again. She didn't see the sudden dip appear in the red bean-bag seat in the corner, or hear the little contented sigh that followed.

"Lena!" Mum shouted, giving her a nudge, "Come on get ready for school!"

Lena rubbed her eyes. It wasn't fair! People who were unfortunate enough to have been disturbed in the night by a stupid barking dog, should be exempt from getting up early.

She stuck her legs out grumpily and climbed down from her bunk, she pulled on her school clothes resentfully, as her Mum went back downstairs. Whose silly idea was it to start school at nine o' clock? Surely it made much more sense to start at eleven? What was the point in turning up for school or work half asleep, and dishevelled? How was anyone supposed to work after eating just a hurried spoonful of cereal and drinking a gulp of coffee? She wondered if she should suggest this time change to her teacher. Grown ups, she'd decided, had no imagination.

She aimed her usual swift kick at an empty bed , lack of uniform strewn across the duvet told her that, as usual, Sam was ready first. Probably eating his breakfast, and commenting on how lazy she was.

She would be glad when Mum and Dad finally finished clearing the spare room, and she didn't have to share with her oh so perfect brother!

She looked at the window, and the curtains that were blowing around. She pulled them open, and looked out at the back garden below. It was funny; she'd closed the window last night. She shrugged, it must have been Mum letting in a bit of 'fresh' air. Flippin' freezing air more like, and that dog was still barking! It would lose its voice at that rate.

She pulled her long copper coloured hair back into a ponytail, as she did so she heard a giggle.
She whirled around. It had come from behind her, in the corner of the room.

"Sam?"
Was he hiding in here? She did a fleeting search of their room, there was no sign of him. Well she couldn't be bothered with his silly games. She grabbed her bag and flung it downstairs.

"Clean your teeth, Lena!" called Mum from downstairs.

"I'm doing it, I'm doing it, give me a chance!" Lena mumbled.
How did her mum know she wasn't going to bother? She snarled at her freckled face in the bathroom cabinet mirror as checked her teeth. She opened the cabinet to grab the toothpaste, piled a load of toothpaste on the brush and shoved it in her mouth for a quick ten-second whiz, she shut the mirrored door again to check her teeth.

Something was there,

"Agh!" She flung herself around to look behind her. She'd seen it in the mirror. A flash of blue, there one instant and gone the next.
There was nothing there now. She frowned at herself.

"You're imagining stuff, Lena, get a grip!"

 She ran down the stairs, stumbling over her little sister's Teletubby. She picked it up and threw it back up the stairs.

"There you go - you like flying don't you, Tinky Winky?"
She smiled, this was all perfectly normal, normal was good, she'd just imagined the blue flash in the mirror.
Her brother Sam was sat there already, all smugness, teeth all done, mop combed so as there wasn't a blonde strand out of place. If he had been hiding upstairs, could he have slipped past her so quickly?

"Come on hurry up!" He rolled his eyes at Lena who was standing thoughtfully in the doorway. Lena was sure that he saved that smug grin especially for her.

She pulled a face at him. In the kitchen her little sister, Missy was at the table, making as much mess as was humanly possible with a bowl of soggy cornflakes.

"Do you want some, Lena?" Mum asked, "You've got five minutes!"

She began pouring the cereal anyway, as there wasn't time for an answer.
Lena sat down and ate her breakfast, though Missy's cornflake-smeared face wasn't doing a great deal for her appetite. Oh well, least it was Friday; she wouldn't have to endure this tomorrow, a nice lie in, that's what she needed.

"Have you got everything you need for today?" Mum asked, piling the bowls into the sink.

"Yes, I put everything in my bag last night like you told me!" Lena fluttered her eyes as if she was an angel.
Mum went into the living room to find the car keys. Seconds later, Sam dashed in the kitchen, a pained expression on his face.

"Have you seen my P.E kit?" He rummaged frantically through the washing basket.

"No, sorry, have you lost it?" Lena mumbled, in her most unhelpful voice. Sam tutted,

"Obviously, or I wouldn't be asking!"

He ran his hands through his hair in frustration. That was the end of the neat mop!
Lena laughed as he dashed back into the living room; she heard him running back upstairs. She finished her breakfast and put on her coat. She helped her sister on with her coat, and went to get in the car, grabbing her mum's handbag on the way.

"Mum, forgotten something?" She passed the bag through to her mum in the driver's seat with a grin.
Her mother swept her hair back into a clip and sighed.

"Oh, thanks, love, I'm all over the place today!"
Lena couldn't help laughing as Sam came running

from the house.

"Keeping everyone waiting?" Lena asked, borrowing Sam's smug grin.

"Oh shut up!" He clambered in the car. Her mother looked in her mirror at the three of them bundled in the back,

"Okay, stop bickering you two, have you got everything now?"

"Yeah!" They both answered like a pair of robots. Missy grinned and thrust her purple robot in the air with a hand covered in cornflake mush.
Mum sighed. They had the same routine every morning. Resolutions to get up early, have everything ready for school and arrive at the gates with time to spare were made every day. Yet come the morning the same thing happened day after day! You would think that after years of practice they could get it right.
"Right! Let's be off then!"
The car pulled away, leaving the driveway empty and the house in silence.

Up in Sam and Lena's bedroom, Lena's crumpled duvet, and her half on, half off bed sheet were straightened out and tucked in with perfect precision. The same thing happened with Sam's bed. The game of Monopoly, which had been left strewn across the floor for about two weeks, because, as they told their mother, 'we're going to finish it', was miraculously sorted out. All the little green houses and red hotels put in the right compartments, and all the counters accounted for; even the little dog which had disappeared under the heavy wardrobe a few months ago, never to be seen again, was back in the box. The rug was straightened out, and the pile of DVDs next to the portable T.V stacked themselves neatly back on the shelf. Dirty clothes picked themselves up and floated off to the washing basket in the bathroom, even Sam's socks, which could be considered a hazardous material.

Then came the sound of a quiet little sigh, and a strange shuffling noise. On Sam's bed, if you had looked closely, you might have noticed a dip in the middle of the mattress for a second. A dip which then moved over to the right and then to the left, almost as if someone had got on the bed, and

were trying to make themselves comfortable.
Not long later, the children's mother came back
home, with little Missy, whom she settled down in
her cot with her cuddly bear, while she got on
with the tidying up.

"I'm just going to make the beds, sweetheart, I
won't be a minute."

She went into Sam and Lena's room but halfway
through the door, she stopped in surprise. It was
tidy! It came as a bit of a shock. She couldn't
remember ever seeing it so tidy.

"Oh."
She smiled; she tilted her head to one side whilst
thinking of the little darlings.

" They tidied up before school; that was so sweet
of them - Amazing, how did they ever have time?"

She closed the bedroom door again, feeling
pleased, although a little confused. A big tidy up
like that would normally take them all day.
Once she had gone back to Missy, the dip on
Sam's bed disappeared, and then the T.V came on,

jumped quickly through a few channels and stopped. It was a programme about endangered species. The sound turned right down, so you would barely have been able to hear it. Then the strange dip appeared again on the bed.

CHAPTER 2

'Cleanliness and chaos'

"That was nice of you!" said Mum later that afternoon, when she picked the weary pair up from school. "Tidying your room this morning, how did you find the time?"

Of course neither Sam nor Lena had a clue what their mum was on about. Beds were a mess; games were all over the floor, not to mention the dirty washing. Perhaps Mum was being sarcastic, trying to say that's what they *should* have done! (Mums were good at that!)

"Oh w-well, you know," stuttered Lena, glancing oddly at Sam, he just shrugged. He might be able to get up in a morning, but the art of tidying up

was something he had yet to master.
They piled in the front door, and hung up their coats; and rushed upstairs to get changed.

"So it really is tidy,." Sam said as he opened the door. There was a sudden noise from the T.V as it flicked off. Lena frowned and pushed him through the door,

"Go on get in there then!"

"What was that noise?" said Sam warily, leaning all his weight back on to Lena to make it difficult for her to shove him.

"Don't know, sounded like the telly!" Lena said, barging passed him. "Get out the way you big baby!"

"It must have been something else, perhaps something dropped off the shelf or something." Sam looked around for the offending object. Lena nodded, stroking her chin thoughtfully, looking as if she had just solved a big mystery.

"Yeah and it had to be Mum who tidied up, she

must have been making a point, you know, that we should have done it!"

She shook his head in bewilderment; it was a mystery to her why people needed things tidy.

"I don't see what's wrong with leaving it in a mess, it can't do you any harm!"

"Well you usually have so many dirty clothes on the floor you might fall in them and never get back out!" He snorted with laughter.

Lena grinned at the image,
 "I guess that could happen, or you trip over your remote control car , go flying and fall out of the window!"
The two of them sat on the bed, laughing at the very idea.

"Or," said Sam between breaths, "you might fall out of bed and land on your creative crystals that you leave all over the floor!"

"Oh ha ha! " said Lena, "That would be pretty painful!" She looked around, feeling a little guilty.

"Maybe we should keep it tidy. It can't be that hard."

"I am tidy!" Sam spluttered indignantly. "It's you!"
Lena pulled a face,
"Whatever."
He had a point.
Sam flopped on the bed. Suddenly he scrambled up again, looking alarmed.

"Did you see that?" he said looking at his bed.

"No, what?" said Lena, "What are you looking at, I can't see anything!"

"The duvet moved!" Sam said, flinging his arms out in front of him and looking at her as if it was obvious. His eyes were wide and he had gone a funny colour.

"Do you think I'm daft?" Lena said, grabbing her blue jumper from the cupboard. She put it on, and looked at Sam with pity.
 Sam was nodding in response to her question.

"Obviously I think you're daft, but I'm being serious, it moved!" Sam said, starting to feel irritated. Lena sighed. He was trying to wind her up, the best thing was to ignore him, that usually worked.

"I'm off downstairs, hurry up - Mum's made tea already!"

She left Sam with a puzzled expression on his face, still staring at his duvet.

Lena sat at the table and made a start on her fish fingers, she grinned as Sam came into the kitchen, now wearing his red spaceship t-shirt.

"Any more moving duvets?" she asked sarcastically, although she knew she had imagined something herself that morning, but it was silly. Now Sam was at it. Sam frowned at her,

"No!" It was annoying how his sister managed to make him feel like an idiot.

"What's all this then?" asked Mum.

"Oh nothing much, just Sam seeing things!" Lena said with a laugh,

"I thought I was seeing things this morning when your room was tidy." Mum said, passing Sam the tomato kecthup. "I hope you're going to do that more often, that would be nice!"

Sam and Lena looked at each other, had Mum really not tidied up for them? They watched her to see if she would laugh at their confused faces, but she didn't. She just seemed happy that they had done something helpful for once.

'Who tidied up?'Lena mouthed silently to a confused Sam, her heart began that thumping again. Sam just shrugged, his face still a bit pale.

After their tea they went back up to their room, Lena stopped abruptly at the door and looked around, puzzled. Sam beside her, mouth open in bewilderment. Their school uniforms, which had been flung on the floor when he got changed, were hung neatly on a hanger on the front of the wardrobe door.

"Ooh, this is weird!" said Lena, crossing her eyes and making a ghostly voice. She knew for a fact that Mum hadn't been upstairs since they came back from school.

"Shh, just sit down and listen for a minute." Sam said.

"Alright keep your hair on!" Lena said pulling a face at him. They sat down on the floor and listened. After a couple of minutes Lena asked in a whisper,
"What are we listening for?"

"Anything!" Sam said abruptly.

"I can't hear *anything*!" Lena said, impatiently,

"Shut up a minute, will you!" Sam said, leaning forward and putting his ear nearer to the bed. Lena looked up to the ceiling in annoyance. The room was so silent, you could have heard a pin drop. Lena smiled to herself; she had just had an idea.
"Argh!" she yelled out suddenly, and backed away to the door.

"What what?" Sam said looking around in a panic. Lena looked at him, wide eyed, with a look of horror and feigning shock; she looked at Sam. His terrified face just made her want to laugh. She couldn't keep it up. Then all of a sudden her expression changed, and she burst out laughing. Sam looked at her, shaking his head, he wasn't amused.

"Oh ha ha, you are so funny, Lena, comedienne of the year award for you!" He looked at Lena who had suddenly stopped laughing, she was looking intently up at the ceiling and Sam sighed,

"Come on, your not funny!" But Lena just shook her head and pointed up at the purple light-shade. She'd noticed it begin to rock, violently from one side to another. They stared at it in silence, not daring to take their eyes away from it as it continued to swing, but started getting slower and slower until it stopped. They stared at it fearfully, eyes wide with alarm.
They stood together, gazing upwards, neither one of them knew what was happening. They felt afraid and began to back away to the door. What could make a light-shade swing violently when

there was no draft?

A worrying sound broke the silence. A kind of tearing noise. It was coming from the ceiling; the wire that was connected to the bulb holder under the shade seemed to be stretching. The paper on the ceiling was tearing under the strain. As they stared, trying to figure out what could be causing it, all of a sudden, the wire snapped, the ceiling paper tore in all directions like cracking ice, and the light-shade plummeted to the floor as if were made of concrete!

There was an almighty thud! Sam and Lena looked at each other in panic. Oh no, they were in for it now!

"YOU TWO!" came a shout from downstairs, "WHAT ON EARTH WAS THAT?" Mum's voice was getting louder, she was coming up!

They made a break for the door. It was too late. Lena stood on the landing, she closed her eyes tightly and covered them with her hands. If she couldn't see the disaster, maybe it would go away. Sam bit his lip, how were they going to explain this one? Mum hurried past them carrying Missy in her arms; she stopped still at the sight that met her eyes. Sam and Lena cringed, waiting for the inevitable fury to unleash itself.

 "Oh ...my...!" for a moment Mum was lost for words,
"What happened?" she asked, in a shocked voice. She looked up at the ceiling and then down at the floor.
The ceiling was a mess, torn paper hanging off, and a hole with dangling wires, where the light fittings were supposed to be! Dust was falling to the floor.
 But it was the floor that was the main problem. There was a dent! That couldn't be a good sign! She covered her mouth partly in distress, and partly in order to prevent herself saying things she may regret, and sank down on the bed.
Sam thought it best not to mention at the time, but as his mum sat down, right next to her, something else sat down, something heavy enough to make a dent. The mattress dipped. Mum didn't notice. Sam nudged Lena; she nodded, without moving her head, which was quite a neat trick. She had already seen it. She said nothing, but went a bit pale and bit her lip as well. Mum was very quiet; unfortunately it was

the calm before the storm.

"Sam, there is a dent in the floor! Please pull back your rug, I want to see the damage!"

She was trying not to shout. Sam obediently did as his Mum said. The rug was very large, it had been put down instead of a carpet, it was to protect the floorboards, which were a very lovely, polished pine. Their Mum and Dad had thought that as the kids were to have the big room, it would be best to cover over the precious flooring. Sam picked up a corner near the door and pulled it back towards the window, revealing the floor underneath.

Mum covered her mouth in horror; she looked almost close to tears.

"I was having such a nice day!" she said quietly.

Sam and Lena sat there with pained expressions. Mum looked at them furiously,

"Okay, come on tell me, WHAT THE HECK WERE YOU DOING?"
Sam and Lena both started talking at once,

"It wasn't us, we didn't do anything, it just fell by itself!"

They looked at her hoping that this would be a reasonable explanation. Sadly, Mum was obviously not the slightest bit impressed with that answer.

"Oh really! What fell exactly? A ten ton elephant?" She snapped. Sam shook his head, eyes wide with protest.

"Honestly, we weren't doing anything, we just heard a creaking noise, and then the whole thing fell down, but I really don't know why it has made a dent in the floor!" He flung his arms out in frustration at his defence, which sounded feeble, even though it was true. Mum nodded,

"I SEE," she said loudly and pointed at the floor, "DO YOU CALL THAT A DENT?" Sam pursed his lips. Lena bent down and looked closer at the floor, as if inspecting it might help. The floorboards were broken. At least four boards were damaged. She looked up at Mum, as innocently as possible.

"Honest Mum, we didn't cause this!"

"How did it happen then?" she demanded, "Someone must have been swinging on the lightshade to have managed to pull the whole thing down!" She alleged, perhaps feeling the culprit might own up if she guessed at the events. She sighed.

'Or something!' thought Lena to herself. Mum, Sam, Missy and herself were definitely not the only ones in the room.

"I still don't see how that happened!" Mum said pointing wildly at the broken floor, disturbing Lena's thoughts. "You can't weigh enough to go through the floor!"

"We don't!" protested Lena. "That's what we've been trying to tell you, it wasn't us!" She threw her arms up in the air so indignantly – and looked at her mother so earnestly, that Lena thought she saw a flicker of a smile at the corner of her mother's mouth.

Then her Mum stood up, coughing and putting her hand to her face. Lena knew it was just an excuse to give her time to force back the smile that was appearing without being asked.

"A-hem, okay we have established you can't have gone through the floor boards, but you must know what happened, you were in the room!" Mum said, finding her angry tone again.

"Err no!" said Sam, his mind searching for a good fib. "We were ...in your room!"

"Yes!" Lena added, "We were ...looking for something! "

"Oh!" said Mum, and then said looking puzzled, "I thought you said you were in here!" They both shook their heads earnestly; fingers crossed behind their backs, this was there last chance to deny all knowledge.
"No, no, definitely not!"

"Well that's just as well then isn't it?" Then she sighed, and looked at their anxious faces, as she did so, Lena and Sam could see her visibly calming down, they could almost see the anger leave her body and fly off through the window, off to somebody else's mother no doubt.

"Oh come on! Not to worry! Nobody is hurt, that's the main thing!" she said in a more relaxed voice.

Lena and Sam nodded, and breathed a sigh of relief, yep – the anger had flown away. Missy, who had been standing quietly by her mother's leg, sucking her fingers and watching while all this was going on, suddenly interrupted,

"Oh Mummee, yook!" (She always said her L's with a 'Y'). She pointed at Sam's bed, a second or so earlier, the mattress had been moving,

Sam and Lena had seen it too. They cringed and watched their mother nervously. Mum looked around.

"What, sweetie?" She asked looking at the bed, "What are you showing me then?"

Lena slipped out of the room and grabbed Tinky

Winky from the landing windowsill.
 She came in the room and shoved it under
Missy's nose. Distraction – that was the thing!
Missy jumped, and her bottom lip quivered as
though she was about to cry, and then she saw
what it was.

"Winky!" Missy gurgled in delight, taking him from
Lena and squeezing him to within an inch of his
life.

Mum watched her and laughed. "Oh well, it
couldn't have been that important then could it?
She took Missy's hand and turned to go. "I think
your mattress looks a little bit worse for wear
Sam. I hope you haven't been bouncing on the
bed!"
Sam folded his arms and gave her a funny look.

"Mum, it's the bottom bunk, I could bounce on it
if I was a foot tall and not too fond of my head!"
Mum pulled a face at him and pretended to
throttle him.

"Smarty pants!" She went to the door, "Right we'll
have to leave the floor for now, I shall have to

break the news to your Dad when he gets back! Leave your rug pulled back and then you can see where not to
walk!"
She closed the door to, and went back downstairs, mumbling about the cost of fixing something that shouldn't need fixing. Lena breathed a sigh of relief; at least the ordeal was over for the moment.

CHAPTER 3

'**Xanleans are everywhere, didn't you know?**'

Sam went to his bed and stood next to the dip in the mattress. He stretched out his hand and went to feel it.
He felt something – but it wasn't the familiar feel of his crisp new space design duvet cover!

"Urgh!" he yelled in horror, snatching his hand away and examining it closely.

"What is it?" Lena asked in alarm. "What are you

doing?"

"You feel!" Sam replied, grabbing her hand and pulling her towards whatever it was.

Lena, not wanting to look lanything other than brave, put her hand out as Sam had done. Her hand just waved about in the air. Then she patted the duvet just to make a point.
"What are you on about, there isn't anything!"
She was irritated, aware that she must look like a right idiot!
"That's 'cause it's moved - it's moved, look!" Sam said excitedly pointing in excitement to a spot a bit further across.
Lena watched, suddenly feeling very nervous. The dip had indeed moved over,

"Go on, see what it feels like!" Sam urged,

"Okay okay!" Lena put her hand out once again. This time she felt something. Her face suddenly scrunched up in horror, she snatched her hand away, her heart racing in panic. "Urgh!" Although she tried to look brave, her heart was pounding like a hammer and she thought she might faint.

She looked at her hand, whatever it was that she had touched - had felt decidedly icky. But there was nothing on her hands, they weren't wet at all. She stood next to Sam and they both gazed at the apparently empty bed.

"What is it?" Lena asked, knowing full well that was a pointless question,
"Maybe one of those horrible poltergeist thingies!" said Sam, gripping Lena's arm and backing away.

"Mmm" said Lena, nervously. She thought for a moment, "It hasn't done anything horrible though! She looked at the damaged floor,
"Just been a bit stupid!" she added.

"It did tidy our room." Sam said, "Not that you can tell now!" he added looking at the floor.

Lena took a deep breath and held out her hand again, this time when she felt it touch her hand she squeezed. Whatever it was squeezed back; it firmly moved her hand up and down.

"Look at that, it's shaking hands with me! It can't

mean us any harm!" She hissed, not doing a very good job of sounding convincing. Sam nodded in encouragement. She tried to let go. It wouldn't. Her hand was in an invisible vice like grip.

"Sam" she said tugging her hand "Sam, it won't let go!" There was urgency in her voice as she started to panic. Sam grabbed on to Lena and pulled as well. They both closed their eyes, and tried with all their might. It just wouldn't leave go. They pulled and pulled, there was a weird kind of stretching noise. But still it wouldn't let go of Lena's hand. Then all at once- it did. Lena and Sam fell backwards with a thud, banging their heads on the wardrobe doors.

"OW!" they yelled out, rubbing their heads.

"That really hurt!" Lena said, almost in tears. Although not quite. Crying in front of her younger brother was a definite no-no. Then all of a sudden, to their amazement and fright, a high-pitched squeal of laughter filled the room.
At the same moment they opened their eyes and they both saw it.

IT was pale blue. IT was quite small, about the size of a five-year-old child. IT had a funny oval face, that was wider than it was long, but a nice face all the same. Then IT smiled. This made its face all the more appealing. Its head was rather large; it had chubby cheeks, and big blue eyes. It had no hair - though considering his skin colour and other features, this hardly seemed strange - and it had tiny little ears that stuck out at the sides of its face like little funnels.

"El. Ohh " It said slowly and carefully. As it moved it's skin wobbled slightly, as if his body was made of jelly. Sam and Lena picked themselves up, and sat a bit nearer. They couldn't take their eyes off the creature.

The creature gazed at them with its huge friendly eyes; it looked a bit confused,

It sat on its bottom, legs outstretched, little chubby legs, its feet tapping together awkwardly.

"Ell oh?" it tried again. Lena lifted her hand and waved slowly, she was in a bit of a daze and her head hurt,

"Hello."

"Who are you?" asked Sam slowly.

"What are you?" added Lena under her breath, finding her voice at last.

It looked puzzled, then it pointed to itself with its long jelly fingers,

"Holl Day! " It spoke slowly saying each syllable with great thought; its big eyes widening, and a huge grin appearing on its face. It looked very pleased with itself. Lena and Sam smiled too, a little warily.
"Hollday " said Lena, "That must be its name!" Sam shrugged,

"Oh well, I suppose that's fair enough. I didn't think he'd be called Josh or Tom!"
He held out his hand to it, and smiled in as much of a friendly way as he could, considering he'd never met a blue jelly creature with no hair before.
"Nice to meet you, Hollday!" Now it was the creature's turn to frown, it looked puzzled.

"Holl e day. Sky!" he said pointing through the window.

"I know!" Sam cried out, as if he'd had a brain wave, which Lena thought was quite rare. He stood up and
went to the window,

"Did you…."He said, pointing to the creature. "… Come from Sky?" he asked pointing up to the sky, and then whooshed his hand down, as if it was flying from the sky in through the window. Lena shook her head,

 "I don't think it understands."

Suddenly the creature nodded vigorously, his blue jelly like cheeks wobbling intensely. It did understand.

"Sky. Holl e day. Marmalachtuloomenaduku.

"What is that, Furbish?" Sam hissed in confusion. Lena shook her head.
"Don't be daft. Shh."

"You are Marmaladumutoo?" asked Lena, trying her best at the name and pointing to the creature, again he nodded excitedly, tapping his blue jelly hands to his chest.

"Marmalachtuloomenaduku."

"Great!" Lena grinned, whispering to Sam, "That's gonna be difficult."

"What are you?" Sam asked slowly, then pressed himself in the tummy "Me- human!" he said, Lena laughed,

"Oh yeah? Could have fooled me!"

Sam tutted at her, and muttered under his breath, "Easily done!"

Marmalachtuloomenaduchu had got off the bed and waddled over to the window.

" Marmalachtuloomenaduchu come Xanlee up high in sky." He said in his strange high-pitched warble. Sam and Lena looked puzzled, "Xanlee? We have never heard of it!" To their surprise, Marmalachtuloomenaduchu giggled, then laughed, then fell to the floor and rolled over uncontrollably, laughing as if he would never stop.

They stared at him; his behaviour was a little alarming but somehow his laughter was very infectious, and seconds later Sam and Lena were giggling helplessly too. After a while, they glanced back at Marmalachtuloomenaduchu whose laughter was now slowing down, and he was catching his breath.
"What's funny?" they asked at last, through their gasps for breath.

"Hu-maans, they- never- hear- abb-out any-thing!" he laughed. "Xanleans everywhere, you know?"

CHAPTER 4

'A Suitcase and a Yoochoo.'

Sam and Lena didn't know whether to laugh or be offended, so they said nothing, but looked at him to see if he would tell them anything else. The little blue entity must have thought that maybe he had been a bit cheeky, he dived under the bed and was quiet.

"Marma...ladutooku!" called Lena, crouching down on the floor and peering under the beds.

"Marmalumoo, what are you doing? Come out, its okay!"

She couldn't see him. She got up and looked at Sam, she shrugged.

"Can't see him!"

Suddenly there was a lot of rummaging noises coming from under the bed.

"Marmalu, what is going on?" Sam said, lying on the floor, and looking under the bunk beds. Before his eyes could become accustomed to the darkness under there, Marmalachtuloomenaduku whooshed back out again.

"At least he responds to Marmalu. I can say that." Sam grinned.

Marmalu reached under the bed, and pulled out a small, grey case. He looked at it with an expression that could only be described as pride, and pointed at Lena and then at the case.

"You look!" he said, slowly. Sam looked at the box, then at Lena, she looked at him and shrugged.

Sam bent down to open the box. He couldn't see any way to open it. It was just sealed, all the way round.

"Come on then we want to see what's in it!" said Lena impatiently.

"I can't open it!" he said and Lena sighed

"Here let me!" she said. She turned the box this way and that, but couldn't find a way to open it! Sam
looked smug,

"Told you!" he said.

Marmalu was grinning again.

"Marmalu open?" he said with a giggle.

"He must think we're a right couple of idiots!" Lena said, flopping on the floor grumpily.

"He'd be right." Sam said, pushing the box to Marmalu disappointedly. Marmalu put his hand on the box, and closed his eyes. Lena and Sam gazed in disbelief as the box began to turn. Slowly and silently it rotated, then a bit faster, seconds later it was spinning around on the spot so fast it made them dizzy. It began to rise up into the air.

Then, all the contents popped out one by one and spun around too. Round and round, faster and faster. Sam and Lena couldn't watch it was going too fast. Then quite abruptly everything came to a halt. The contents of the box piled themselves neatly in a stack on the floor; right in front if them.

"Wow!" Lena said. "How did you do that?" Marmalu shrugged and smiled,

"Marmalu clever!" He said simply. They all laughed, his expression was so funny, and the way he made everything seem so simple. He's even said his name the way they'd shortened it. He was clever.

"Well OK!" Sam shuffled on his knees towards the neat pile. "Right let's see, what have we got here."

He reached for a circular shaped piece of something that looked like the lid from a baked bean can. It was like metal, with lots of grooves going across it. As his hand touched the object, it immediately expanded. Sam jumped . It stretched again until it was the size of a piece of notepaper, and then words appeared as if by magic, illuminated on its surface.

Lena was watching in fascination.

"It looks like writing!"

The illuminated shapes appeared to be words but nothing they were used to, ibut a mixture of symbols and shapes.

Sam nodded, he looked at Marmalu, as he picked it up again.

"We don't understand!" he said pointing at the writing, shaking his head and shrugging.

"What do I do now" He whispered to Lena, Marmalu wouldn't understand.
To his surprise, Marmalu did seem to understand what he was on about. He took hold of Sam's other hand, and placed it on the other side of the strange object.
"Now-see!" Marmalu said.

Sam gazed at the illuminated tin can note in amazement. Before his eyes the strange writings erased and suddenly appeared to be written in

English.
"It's English!" He grinned in excitement, showing Lena, she put her hands on the object too, then Lena read out loud:

"Dear Lena, Sam and Missy," she began, in astonishment,

"What? Let me see that again!" Sam said pulling it towards him in disbelief, "It can't be addressed to us!" Lena pulled it back,

"Dear Lena, Sam and Missy,
Thank you very much for agreeing to have Marmalachtoolumenaduku to stay with you. We are going through some very difficult times here on Xanlee. It isn't safe for the children. We very much appreciate what you are doing.

We hope you can teach him some of your language and some of your ways, while he is staying with you.

He has lots of things to teach you!

Thank you again for what you are doing.

With kind regards

Jayle and Kahl.

At the sound of the last two names, Marmalu jumped up, he reached over for the letter which Lena was holding, as soon as he touched it, the writing returned to the language of Xanlee. Marmalu looked at it, and smiled.

"Marmalu stay?" he asked, his big wide eyes looking at them soulfully.

Lena just nodded, though she was very confused.

"I don't get it!" said Sam. "We've never even heard of Xanlee!"

"Mm, I know what you mean. What does it mean, thank you for agreeing to have Marmalu to stay? We don't understand." Lena said as she looked at Marmalu, hoping for an explanation, but none arrived. Instead Marmalu just shrugged.

"Ha! Look at that! He's learning your ways already, Sam!" Lena grinned.

However, Lena felt that Marmalu knew exactly what was going on. She could tell by his expression. What was it Mum called that expression? Oh yes, sheepish, Marmalu looked sheepish!

She looked at Sam hoping for a second opinion, but the nosy article was busy delving in the box,

"What else is there?" he enthused, reaching out for a small ball, which had also been in the case.

"What's this?" he asked, shaking it about.

"A ball?" Lena said sarcastically. "Just a wild guess!" She took it and bounced it against the wall. Instead of springing back towards her hands like a normal ball would, it appeared to stick to the wall by invisible glue then it began an amazing transformation.

It shimmered and spread out until became a large circle, it rippled like a stream. Then a spectrum of colours filtered through.

"What is it?" Sam whispered, transfixed.
Marmalu pointed at the children's TV.

"What? It's a TV? Is that what you mean?" Lena asked.

"TV" Marmalu nodded, he pointed up to the shimmering circle of colour,
"Marmalu TV"

"Wow!" said Sam. "That's your TV? So much better than digital!" Lena looked up,

"That's so cool! How does it work?" she asked Marmalu.
Marmalu was already making it work. He stood in front of the 'TV' and gazed at it unblinkingly. It began to take shape, and before their eyes there appeared animals, or creatures of some kind, more like dinosaurs.
They watched in amazement, the dinosaurs creatures looked so real!

Lena's heart began to race. She looked at Sam a little uneasily. They had never seen anything like it. The creatures were as real as they would be looking at them at a zoo. The images of them weren't life size of course, they were small , but so real, as if you could reach out and pluck them from the air! They weren't contained in a square box, but walked around naturally as if on a cushion of air.

"What are they?" Sam asked reaching up into the shimmering vision. It rippled as his hand went nearer.

"Earth had Nesaurs!" Marmalu replied mysteriously, pointing at the lifelike creatures.

"What do you mean?" Sam shook his head to show that he didn't understand.

"They go to Xanlee, before Earth go boom!" He puffed out his cheeks and made a funny noise.

"Wow!" said Lena "They really are Dinosaurs? Our dinosaurs? She took a little step closer, and peered at the dinosaurs. A diplodocus swept past them reaching for a particularly green leaf. Lena was enthralled, she could almost be there, in this miniature world. She was sure she could even smell the foliage as the diplodocus munched.

"They are on Xanlee!" she whispered, "that's

amazing, how can it be possible?"

"That doesn't make sense!" said Sam "Everyone knows a comet wiped out the dinosaurs years ago.!"

"Just because they are on this 'TV' thing , it doesn't mean they are actually on Xanlee!"

"Yeah right, listen to you! A few minutes ago, we would never have known, there even existed a place like Xanlee! How can we possibly know what Marmalu has on his planet" Lena said, still gazing at the life like dinosaurs.

Sam didn't feel like arguing, he knew she had a point. He stood next to her as she watched the dinosaurs , it was truly amazing. He reached out to them.

"It's almost as if you could touch them !" he said "Like they are actually here!" Sam snatched his hand back, the look of surprise frozen on his face. He looked at his hand again, checking it was all intact. He seemed to be doing that a lot today.

"What?" Lena asked him, "What is it?"

"You can, you can touch them, really - you can feel their skin!"

Marmalu was watching the two of them in amusement, he burst out laughing in his funny high pitched voice.
Lena and Sam jumped. The sight of his face all scrunched up, his big smile stretched across his face, was very infectious, they laughed too.

"You are so lucky to have a TV like that!" said Sam.

"What's in here?" Lena asked Marmalu, as she forced herself away from the 'TV'. She cleared her throat. She'd obviously never seen a dinosaur before, only in books and a skeleton in a museum once. She felt very moved that the creatures had been rescued. They were OK, somewhere a long way away. She sniffed.

She picked up a small red rectangular basket, Marmalu took it in glee,

"Yoochoo!" he said, he opened the basket. He

took something from the basket and held it close to him. Whatever it was he obviously loved it to bits!

"Can we see?" Lena asked, Marmalu opened his hands a little so Lena could peep in. She looked at the thing
in his cupped hands, and jumped back in surprise.

"Sam, why don't you look?"

Sam looked suspicious,

"Why. Is it gross?" He asked nervously.

"No! Go on!" said Lena, giving him a nudge.

Sam gave her a look, "If this is something gross, you're in for it!" Lena gave him a shove,

"Just look!"

Sam went over to the box Marmalu cradled in his arms. He looked in, warily. Whatever it was, it was alive.
"Whoa" he said in amazement, That is brilliant!"

he looked back at Lena, "Isn't it?"

Lena nodded.

They sat down and watched as Marmalu carefully took out the little creature from the box. It was an amazing looking thing,

"What is he, exactly?" Sam asked quietly

"Maylonn baby!" said Marmalu. "Yoochoo!"

Sam and Lena fell silent, they were lost for words. They had barely got over the shock of having an alien in their bedroom! Now they had an alien with a pet . They watched as the little thing gazed lovingly at Marmalu, its warm brown eyes bright and full of curiosity. Then it looked around warily. It was unlike any other creature they had seen in their books and encyclopaedias at school. More like a crazy invention someone might post online! It was a little thing, about the size of a hamster, it was pale pink in colour, Its skin looked soft; not scaly like a dinosaur, nor was it furry like a mouse, it just looked soft, like a peach. It had a lovely face, with big brown eyes, and a little nose. Yoochoo gazed all around, it began to make a funny whistling sound. It looked at Sam and Lena for a brief second, then jumped back and huddled itself against Marmalu.

"Oh, it's afraid of us!" said Lena, disappointed. She felt in her pocket and brought out a bit of chocolate. "Ah! I thought I had some left!" She held out a tiny piece in her hand. It was a bit squishy. She offered it to Yoochoo. The baby alien looked at the chocolate longingly, the all of a sudden, she leapt out of Marmalu's arms, and jumped onto Lena's knee. Lena almost jumped out of her skin. Marmalu laughed, making a weird gurgling noise.

"He like choc-lot!"

Lena gave the Maylonn the chocolate, it sniffed it in glee, then took it in it's paw. It put the chocolate in it's mouth, then to Lena's delight it settled itself down on her knee. It began to make a purring noise, like a cat, but louder as if there was a mini generator in there, revving itself up.

"Isn't she gorgeous!" said Lena. "I can't believe it!"

"Well it will make a great 'What I did at weekend' story at school on Monday!" laughed Sam.

"Marmalu have school, but Marmalu on hol- i- day!" gurgled Marmalu in delight. "No work for Marmalu!" he giggled, his chubby little body rocking uncontrollably. Lena laughed too. She cuddled the little creature in her lap, who was snuggled against Lena, still snoozing. Lena stroked its head gently.

"Oh, Yoochoo is lovely, you are lucky!"

All of a sudden Yoochoo sat up, eyes widened in alarm and she listened carefully. Then she got up and ran to Marmalu, jumping into his arms and huddling into a ball.

"Some one coming!" Marmalu said.

Sam and Lena looked at each other in panic. It was Dad on his way up.

"Quick Marmalu, hide!"

Marmalu looked confused.

"Hide, hide quickly!" Lena pleaded. She pulled Marmalu by the hand, and she and Sam bundled him under the bed as best they could.

"Hello Kids, I hear you've had a hectic day!" came Dad's voice. They heard him go into his room.

"Sam!" hissed Lena "Do something! He'll be in here, in a second.

She nodded towards Marmalu's feet, which were sticking out from under the bed. Sam looked around in panic for something to cover them up with. He grabbed his nightgown from the bedroom door and flung it on top of Marmalu's feet,.

"Hey!" gurgled Marmalu with a giggle. "What doing?"

"Shhh!" said Sam, he sat on his bed and picked up a book, as Dad came in.

"Come on then, tell me, what have you been doing? Mum says there has been an accident."

"Yes!" said Lena. "But we didn't cause it, honestly!"

Dad bent down and looked at the floor boards. He looked up at the ceiling.

"It just doesn't make sense!" he said, "How could the light fitting cause this much damage. It looks more like something rather heavy fell from the ceiling!"

He looked questioningly at the two children, who gazed back with the most innocent looking expressions they could find. He shook his head and sighed.

"Well it looks as if someone will be doing a spot of D I Y!" Sam and Lena nodded sympathetically.

"Right I'll leave you to it!" said Dad opening the door, "Sam, is that your night-gown on the floor? Pick it up please!" he said on his way out.

"Err okay!" stuttered Sam, he made as if to pick up his gown, until he heard Dad close the bedroom

door.
He looked at Lena.

"Phew! That was close!"

"Tell me about it!" agreed Lena.

Lena picked up Sam's night gown. There was
nothing underneath.

"Marmalu?" she called. She could hear a giggle.
She knelt down and peered under the bed.
"Marmalu?" He was nowhere to be seen.
She got up again, Sam was looking amused,

"Can't find him eh?" Lena shook her head.

"He is invisible again!" he whispered to Lena.

"Well why didn't he just say he would make
himself invisible, instead of us having to mess
about hiding him?" Lena asked in a hushed voice.
Sam put his finger over his mouth, "Shh!" he
gestured. He walked to the door then said in a
loud voice.

"Well if Marmalu's gone, we might as well go and play downstairs!"
Lena followed him, she just knew this would work, she felt a giggle welling up inside her.

"Marmalu here!" said Marmalu in a panic, appearing in a shimmer on Sam's bed. Yoochoo still cradled in his arms.

"Don't leave Marmalu!" He warbled looking upset, Sam looked at him feigning surprise,

"Oh there you are!" he said. "We thought you'd gone!"

"No, no Marmalu not gone, no where to go!" He looked upset.

"You not want Marmalu to stay?" he asked.
Lena suddenly felt guilty for laughing; he looked so sad. She sat down next to him and put her arm around him.

"We were just kidding!" she said. "We didn't say you couldn't stay!" Sam stood in front of Marmalu not knowing what to say. Lena frowned at him.

Sam looked thoughtful,

"Marmalu, what do you mean you have nowhere to go, can't you go back home?"
Marmalu thought for a moment, then shook his head.

"Marmalu not allowed, not now, not safe!"
Sam looked at Lena,

"Maybe there is some sort of war going on!" he said. Lena laughed,

"Sam! What do you think it is, Star Wars?"

"Well it could be, what do we know, what do we know about anything? In fact do you realise that we have proof of extra terrestrial life forms, sitting here in our bedroom? There are planets out there that our scientists and all the rest of the brainy bunch know nothing about! We are in fact, one step ahead!" He pulled a serious Sherlock Holmes-like impression.
Lena looked at him like he was mad.

"Hey? You've lost me, one step ahead of what?"

Sam rubbed his head in frustration,

"Don't you watch T.V? There's always some space mission going to Mars or Venus or wherever, looking for signs that planets would be able to support life. We know more than anyone, more than, you know, N A S A!"

Lena nodded, "Yeah I see your point, but so what?"
Sam shrugged,

"I don't know yet, but it makes me feel a bit smug!"
Lena laughed,

"You, smug?" She said in mock astonishment
She gave Marmalu another hug, "Yeah, we can be sooo Smug!" They all laughed.

"Marmalu stay?" he asked above the sound of laughter, a huge grin on his chubby face. Sam and Lena nodded,

"YES" Even Yoochoo squeaked in delight.

Sam made a false coughing sound.

"A hem! By the way Marmalu, I think you have been trying to avoid the issue, by showing us all this weird stuff. But I think you broke our floor!" Marmalu looked sheepish. Sam and Lena looked at him, he covered his mouth.

"Oops!" he mumbled apologetically.
They all started to laugh.

"Marmalu fix!" He said simply.

CHAPTER 5

'Xanlee'

That night Marmalu told them all about Xanlee.
Lena was in bed looking at the ceiling. Sam was
showing off on his games console. Marmalu had
opted to sleep on the bean bag. It was that or the
floor, so it wasn't a difficult decision. He put
Yoochoo in his little house and put him under
Sam's bed, so he wouldn't be seen.
Marmalu brought out the 'reality display' or TV as
they called it. Sam put his game on pause.
Xanlee looked amazing. Like everything you ever
wanted on holiday, sun, sea, sand, swimming
pools. And grown ups -what did they always

want? Scenery, the scenery was beautiful, even Sam, who was always unimpressed, could see that Xanlee was pretty much perfect. Green mountains, with beautiful cascading water falls. Exotic looking trees and plants.

"Wow!" said Lena, quite moved. "That looks gorgeous!" Sam was gazing up at the display, lost for words.
Marmalu had grinned, obviously proud of his home.

"Glad you like!" he said "But what is not there?" he asked. Sam looked confused.

"what do you mean?"
Marmalu stood up, and pointed up at the display,

"See, not there."

"There is something missing?" Lena asked.

"Yes yes, something missing!" said Marmalu.

Sam gazed at the display, then said in a low voice, as if knowing that what he had realised meant bad news for Xanlee. "People"

Marmalu nodded. Sam and Lena were quiet for a few minutes. Sam sighed. "What has happened, Marmalu?"
Marmalu smiled.

"Do not worry, it is not so bad. People gone safe place. There is a war. Lots of Marmalus come here, Xanleans everywhere"

"So there are lots like you, here?"

"On earth, not here, me only one in this place!"

"But what is the war about?"

 Marmalu screwed up his face, trying to think of a way to describe what was happening.
"A new place being made, on another planet. The ones who made it are called Deridon, and they want people of Xanlee to move there."

"What for?"
Marmalu shrugged,

"We don't know."

They all sat around for a while quietly. It was a lot to take in. Aliens. Planets. Wars. What else was left?
They talked quietly for hours, until they finally went to sleep. Marmalu turned himself invisible, and curled up on the bean bag, until he was peacefully dreaming.

CHAPTER 6

'A disturbance'

Lena rubbed her eyes blearily.
"What time is it?" It was still dark.

"What is that noise?" Someone was saying. It was Mum, she was looking for something in their room.

"That flippin' noise has been going on for ages, what is it? It's woken us up!" She whispered. Lena sat up.

"I don't know" She listened. Beep Beep Beeeeep. Beep beep beeeeep. It went. Over and over. Lena, who had momentarily though it was just another night, suddenly remembered everything.
Marmalu! She thought in a panic. Her Mum was about to stand on the bean bag! Lena jumped up, and scrambled down the bunk bed ladders. She had just realised where the sound was coming from. She reached under the bed, and pulled out Marmalu's communicator.

"Well what is it?" Mum asked.

"Err its just Sam's game, he left it on!" she said. "I'll turn it off, I just need to look for the button.

Luckily for her, Mum wasn't in the mood for a chat, she shook her head. "Please just try and turn it off its driving me mad! Honestly the only person it hasn't woken up is Sam!"
Lena nodded, wondering what Mum would think if she knew there was another person in the room. Mum shut the door.
Lena sat up in her bed looking at Marmalu's communication board. It was beeping still. How was she supposed to shut this thing up, she

looked all over it for a button or switch. As she did so, the board lit up, its words were in English, as they had been the day before when she touched it.

'Message for Marmalachtuloomenaduchu' it said. It stopped beeping. Lena looked over to where she thought Marmalu was sleeping. She couldn't get him up now, Mum might come in again! She tucked the board under her pillow, and laid back down. It was difficult to sleep. She thought of all the things that had happened since yesterday. Thoughts tumbled over and over in her head, until they made no sense, and she was fast asleep once more.

"Guess what?" Sam said next morning, "I had this really weird dream, Mum came in and found Marmalu, he was talking in his own language, he was just kind of beeping all the time." Lena burst out laughing,

"You'd sleep through an earthquake you would ."

"What do you mean?" said Sam, puzzled. Lena told him about the night's events.

"Where's Marmalu?" Sam said going over to the bean bag, he reached out. Marmalu was there. "He must be asleep still."

"How long do you think he'll sleep for?" Lena asked. Sam shook his head,

"No idea" Lena went to brush her teeth and get dressed in the bathroom.

"Marmalu!" Sam said "Marmalu, wake up!"

 Marmalu stirred, Sam heard him making yawning sounds. Slowly he re appeared. He grinned at Sam.

 "Forgot where I was!" he gurgled. Sam laughed, Marmalu was so funny sometimes!
Lena came back in,

"Did you tell him?" she asked, when she saw Marmalu was up.

"Tell what?" Marmalu asked, in his broken English.

Lena stood on the ladders and pulled the board

out from under the pillow.

"There was a message for you! It came last night! It woke Mum up and everything! What is it?"

She gave it to Marmalu.

"OK, Lena, give him a chance!" said Sam in a tone that got on her nerves. She pulled a face at him. Marmalu read the message. "Mum wants to say hello, and am I okay, and all that. She wants to know if programme is a good idea?"

"What programme? Something on TV?" Marmalu gurgled his laugh.

"Exchange programme." He said through his giggles.
Lena held her hand to her head,

"ooh, it just gets better!"

"What are you on about Marmalu? Make sense!" Sam said.

"Shut up Sam, I bet you wouldn't make sense in his language!" Lena said. Sam fell silent, he knew she had a point.

"Exchange!" said Marmalu. "You know, I come here," he pointed to the floor, "You come there!" he pointed out of the window. Lena and Sam looked at each other in astonishment. They gazed at Marmalu, open- mouthed. Marmalu looked puzzled.

"You OK?" he asked coming closer, and looking into their faces worriedly. Lena nodded, and looked at Marmalu, she spoke in a hushed voice, hardly believing what she was about to say.

"You mean, maybe we could go to Xanlee?" she asked at last. Marmalu nodded, as if it was no big deal, "Not yet though, it not safe yet. Mame said."

Sam shook his head

"We couldn't do that, there is no way to get to Xanlee, I mean it isn't even in our solar system."

 Lena tutted, why did Sam have to be so negative, he could be such a spoil sport!

"Yeah right, Sam, if you say it can't be done, then it can't be done! But answer me this, if it can't be done, how did Marmalu get here?"

Sam shrugged his shoulders, he looked at Marmalu thoughtfully. It was all so unbelievable, yet how could he be surprised by the possibilities of space travel when there was an alien standing in his bedroom! Well two aliens, not forgetting Yoochoo, who at that moment was running over Marmalu's arm across his back and down the other arm.
Marmalu was giggling.

"You are funny! Make things seem so hard!"

"So it isn't difficult then, it really is no big deal?" asked Sam. Marmalu beamed all over is funny face,

"No big deal!" He repeated Sam's phrase.
Lena sat down,

"Do you mean that your Mum and Dad actually think it would be good for us to come and stay with you?"

Marmalu thought for a moment trying to make sense of what Lena had said, he was getting much better at this 'English language' but it could be difficult at times. He nodded,

"Not just you, lots of children!"

"And lots of your friends will come to Earth I suppose?" Sam said. It made sense, well it would have done if they were talking about an exchange between schools in England and France. But Earth and another planet, a planet that no one knew existed! Did that make any sense?
Marmalu was wriggling around, it was as if he couldn't sit still for a second.

"It would be great!" Lena said. "I just can't believe it! I mean what about our parents, they wouldn't want us jetting off to the far reaches of space!"

"Well" Marmalu said, rolling over on to his wobbly tummy, "If the children agree, then the parents won't know!" Lena was confused,

"Sorry I don't get it!"

"You can be there and back before they know it! Xanleans wont want your grown ups to know about Xanlee, they might try to take it away. It has happened before!" Marmalu said slowly.

"So you're saying that as long as the kids agree, and keep it to themselves, it could all go ahead, we could go to visit Xanlee?"
Marmalu grinned
"That's right, you're clever!" Sam pulled a face at him,
"You're catching on, Marmalu, sarcasm now, is it?" he laughed.
"Wow, wait till I tell my friends about this!" said Lena,

"Shh!" Sam got up and went to the door, "It's mum!"

Before he'd even finished speaking, Marmalu dived under the bed, taking Yoochoo with him.

CHAPTER 7

'A stressful day out'

"Kids, are you going to stay up here all day?"

Lena jumped up, "No, we were just coming. "

Mum glanced around the room, "Something odd in here!" she said suspiciously, "What are you doing? Sam you're not even dressed, come on get a move on!"

Sam grabbed some clothes and went to the bathroom.

"Dad and I thought you might like to go out somewhere today?"

"Yeah!" came a voice from under the bed.
"What was that?" Mum asked,

"Yeah, great idea!" Lena said, doing a pitiful job of trying to put Mum off the scent. Mum laughed at her face,

"Well you certainly seem in a good mood! Lets hope you and your brother can get on today, without any bickering!"

"That would just be weird!" Lena grinned. Mum shook her head and sighed,

"Okay, come on then, get some breakfast and we'll get going." She closed the door.

Lena flopped down on the bean bag with a heavy sigh.

"Sorry Marmalu, you'll have to stay here on your own today." She said apologetically.
Marmalu jumped up with a wobble, eyes wide.

"No Marmalu not stay, Marmalu come too!" Lena looked alarmed. "No Marmalu we can't let you come!" she scrambled to her feet, as Marmalu was heading for the door. "Please Marmalu just sit down for a second." She squeezed through the door so as not to let Marmalu out. "Sam!" she called, "Sam, hurry up!"

"What what? Asked Sam, finally coming out of the bathroom. He looked at his sister in amusement. "Why so stressed?" he asked annoyingly.

"It's Marmalu!" Lena hissed, pulling on the door, Marmalu was obviously pulling hard from the other side.

"Marmalu wants to come!" he wailed.

"He wants to come?" said Sam, "Well tell him he can't!"

"Ooh!" said Lena, feigning shock, "You're so smart!" she thumped her head with her free hand. "Why didn't I think of that?"

Sam frowned, "Okay so you've tried that!" He looked at her thoughtfully, as Marmalu's wailing got louder,

"Maybe he could come!" he said with a shrug.

"Are you mad?" asked Lena, getting even more worked up. "And give me a hand with this door!" Sam pulled on the door also. Marmalu was very strong.

 "All I'm saying is we can't leave him here, and if we don't shut him up Mum will be up here! We'll make sure he stays invisible!"
Lena thought about it,

"Yes but even so! We will be driving around with an alien in the car, that's a bit freaky, don't you think?"

"Well , who's to now?" Sam answered with a smug grin. He let go of the door, Lena let go too, with a sigh, she shook her head in distress.

"I must be mad!" she mumbled.

Marmalu was still pulling on the door, as the two children let go, he continued to pull, and fell backwards with an enormous thud.

"Ow, Marmalu bump" he wailed looking close to tears. Sam tried to pull him up, trying not to laugh.

"Give me a hand, Lena!" Lena grabbed Marmalu's other hand.
"Blimey, Marmalu how much do you weigh?" The two of them struggled to pull him up. "No wonder you broke the floor boards! You must weigh a ton!"

Marmalu was embarrassed. In fact, thought Lena, he would have been blushing if it wasn't for the fact that his skin was blue and it wouldn't show. Marmalu looked at the floor.

"I said would fix!" he said and smiled.
Lena looked at the floor,

"Well how can you?"
Sam pulled back the carpet so they could see the broken floorboards. The both stared in astonishment.

"You already fixed it?" Lena said, "How? When?" they couldn't believe it. Sam bent down and felt the floorboards. There was no sign of a join or anything. They were just perfect.

Marmalu was obviously enjoying their admiration. He chucked.

"No big deal!" and he shrugged, as if he was trying to imitate Sam.

"That's very good !" said Lena and laughed at Sam's indignant face.
There was a shout from downstairs.

"Are you two ready?" Dad called.

"Oh no! How do we explain this?" Lena said, pulling the rug over the floorboards.

"Well it has to be easier to explain you fixed something, than to explain you broke something!" said Sam reasonably.

"Yeah, sure!" said Lena. "Come on, we'll sort it out later. We have to go!"

"Coming Dad!" they shouted.

"Marmalu come" asked their new friend, his big blue eyes looking beseechingly at them, like a little puppy.

"Come on then, but you have to promise to stay invisible!" said Sam.
Lena followed them out of the bedroom.

"Phew!" she said to herself, running her hands through her hair. "At this rate, with all this stress, I'll be grey by Monday!"
They all trooped out of the front door, an invisible Marmalu sandwiched between them.

"He's like a jelly sandwich!" Sam said, and Lena burst out laughing. They climbed into the car, still giggling, while Dad locked the front door. Missy was strapped in her baby seat, behind the passenger seat. Sam sat next to her, and Marmalu and Lena followed. It was a bit of a squeeze. Marmalu was rather a chubby alien!

To Lena's horror, Missy looked right at Marmalu, or where Lena assumed Marmalu was, as she couldn't actually see him for herself.

"Who?" Missy shouted, pointing her little baby hand at Marmalu. "Who?" She said again.

Sam looked alarmed. He stared at Lena, hoping she'd know what to do. She replied with a startled shrug.

"Who?" Missy demanded, kicking her little legs in annoyance.

"Who's what, honey?" Mum said, from the front seat. Marmalu kept his mouth shut for once. Mum turned herself round to look at Missy.

"Who?" Missy was still saying. She had done this last week when one of Sam's friends had come for tea. She liked to know everybody's name. How could she see Marmalu? Lena and Sam looked at Mum and shrugged. Mum smiled at Missy,

"I don't know, sweetheart, do you mean Sam?"
Missy, of course shook her head vigorously and
frowned, sticking out her bottom lip.

"Well I don't know what you mean! " She handed
Missy her cup of milk. Missy took it gratefully.
Soon they were on their way, Missy kept glancing
at Marmalu suspiciously. Marmalu could see she
was looking right at him. He smiled at her
reassuringly. Sam leaned over and whispered to
Missy.

"Marmalu!" he said, then he put his finger over
his lips. "Marmalu a secret, shh!" he said. Missy
giggled.

 "Marmu!" She copied and Sam nodded. "Shh" he
said and smiled at her. Missy was happy with that,
she soon fell asleep.
Sam looked at Lena in relief.

"Phew!" he gestured wiping his brow with his
hand.
Lena nodded.
"How did she see him?" She asked silently.

Marmalu gave her a nudge. "Not worry!" he whispered. "Shh!" Sam and Lena said simultaneously.

They were going to a theme park. Mum and Dad had wanted to surprise them. They had been once before, and as soon as Lena saw the signs on the motorway exit she knew where they were going. They cheered and started talking excitedly.

"I'm going on 'Death Defyer' this time!" Sam stated determinedly.

"You're probably not tall enough, shorty!" teased Lena.

Dad parked the car, and they all piled out. Mum paid the tickets, and they ran through the gates in excitement.

"What shall we do first?" asked Sam.

"What is this place?" whispered Marmalu, gazing around in wonder. "Why is so much screaming?" he asked, looking alarmed, as a roller-coaster ride thundered past above their heads; carrying dozens of thrill seekers waving their arms in the air like lunatics.

"It's just a ride, Marmalu, just for fun!" Lena said, sensing the worry in his voice.

"Right kids where to first?" asked Dad, as Mum came up carrying Missy.
"I think I'll take Missy to the little tots place over there. You three go and do whatever, I'll stay with Missy. Then it's your turn to watch, and I'll have a go!" she said giving Dad a nudge.

 "OK!" he said with a smile. "See you in a bit!"

They all headed off to the 'Darkness' ride. Marmalu clung on to Sam's jacket so he didn't get lost. He was suddenly very nervous. So many aliens in one place. He was very glad most of them couldn't see him. He had noticed however, babies and tiny tots pointing over at him and smiling, or crying. Luckily nobody had taken any notice. Why hadn't his parents warned him that Earth toddlers would be able to see him even when he was invisible? It made him feel very vulnerable.
They joined the queue at the ride. Marmalu

looked around in awe. Humans were obviously enjoying all this. He watched as the roller coaster train went by, full of laughing faces and shrieks of joy. He giggled. He kept an eye on Sam and Lena's Dad, just making sure he didn't see him or hear him. Luckily there was that much going on, their Dad didn't have time to notice that Sam's jacket was puffed out backwards. If he had looked closely, it would have looked as though somebody invisible was holding it! Which was, of course, true!

Soon they all got on the ride. Marmalu squashed himself between Sam and Lena, and the ride set off.

"Here we go, hold on tight!" Dad said, as the carriage entered the tunnel. They chugged up the dark tunnel slowly. As they climbed higher and higher.

"This not thrilling!" Marmalu whispered to Lena. She giggled

"Just you wait!" Almost immediately as she had said it the carriage took a down turn.

"Aaaaagh!" shrieked Marmalu. Sam and Lena screamed all the louder so no one would here his high-pitched scream. The carriage plunged its passengers downwards into the deep darkness and before they could get their breath, twisted and turned, over and up, then down and around, until they could see the light. The ride came to a halt back where they had started.

"Wow, that was pretty good!" Sam and his Dad agreed.
They climbed out .

"Did you like it, Marmalu?" whispered Lena.

"Err" came the gurgling response. Marmalu was lost for words.

"I think he's speechless!" laughed Lena.

"Marmalu? Never!" They patted him on the back, he was trembling, in an extra wobbly sort of way.

"You okay, Marmalu?" asked Lena.

"That was goood!" Marmalu said, at last.

They followed their father to the next ride.

"I thought you space travellers would be used to all that g-force!" said Lena.

"Not like that!" said Marmalu. "Much quieter. No wobbles!"

"Really? That's amazing, you mean you can travel all that way so fast, and you don't get thrown around?" Sam was intrigued. "So these rides are worse that space travel?"

"Mm, more throw about!" gurgled Marmalu. "What doing now?"

"We are going on Death Defyer!" Sam said, flinging his arms out, and pointing up at the ride above them.
Marmalu sighed. "Marmalu watch!"

"Don't you want to come with us, Marmalu?" Lena asked.

"Marmalu watch." Lena was a bit worried, she

didn't like to leave him.

"Well OK, but stay there, don't go anywhere or you'll get lost!" She took him by the hand and led him to a nearby bench. Now stay there, and don't make yourself visible, whatever you do! Do you know what I mean?" Marmalu nodded. Lena waited for an answer.
"Marmalu, are you nodding, because I can't see you?"
Marmalu laughed.

"I stay here, promise!"

"OK! I won't be long!" Lena patted him on the head, and went off to catch up with Sam and her Dad. They joined the queue. Sam and Lena looked down at the bench, they couldn't see anything. Marmalu must still be invisible.
"Oh no!" groaned Lena. "Do you see who I see?"
Sam looked to where she was pointing.
"Oh, heck, James!"

CHAPTER 8

'Unwanted attention'

James Whiting was the biggest creep at school, he was such a teacher's pet, always telling tales on everyone.

"I didn't know James had a little brother!" Said Lena looking at a little boy with James and his mum, he looked about three.

"He's gonna see Marmalu! He'll tell James and

then James will tell...the whole world! We have to tell him to move!" Sam and Lena turned around. There was a queue a mile long behind them. No way through, too many grown ups and big kids!

"We're next kids!" Dad shouted excitedly, watching the group of people in front of him being strapped into their seats.

"Oh!" Lena looked around in panic, "What do we do?" Sam was watching what was happening down at the bench. James and family were only going to sit down and eat their packed lunches!

"We're too late, oh, Marmalu be careful!" Lena said, gritting her teeth and cringing.

"Come on Lena, we aren't even on the ride yet!" Dad said, with a laugh. Lena smiled, well it was more of a grimace than a smile. Sam was leaning over the wooden barrier trying to see James.

"See anything?" Lena hissed under her breath, not wanting her Dad to ask what they were looking at.

"They're just sitting, maybe Marmalu has moved, he wouldn't want to get sat on!"

"Who wouldn't what? What are you two looking at?" Dad asked, leaning over them to see what was making them so curious. "isn't that boy from your school? Is that why you are staring at him?" Dad nudged Lena with a laugh, Lena pulled a horrified face,

"Dad, please, be serious. James? He's mean!" Dad held up his hands,

"OK OK I apologise! Now come on, are we going on this thing or not?" Sam and Lena shrugged, they walked up to their seats next to their Dad. They were strapped in and the ride began to start up. They rose up slowly, high above the ground.

"Look, there's your Mum!" said Dad. They waved frantically at their Mum and Missy, Mum didn't notice, she was chatting to someone. It was Mrs Whiting, James' mum. Before they had chance to comment. The ride whooshed downwards taking their breath away. It threw them around and around. Then it went back up again flinging its passengers outwards, so they almost felt they were going to fall from their seats.

Sam and Lena screamed. It was so fast. Lena was beginning to feel decidedly sick.

Down below, their Mum was having a nice little chat with James and his mum. She had sat down beside them on the edge of the bench, with Missy on her knee. Missy stared at James' little brother. They both giggled, they started babbling away in their own language as toddlers do.

"So how are you, James, are you enjoying your day out?" Mum asked. James just nodded.

"He's sulking, I wouldn't let him on that ride over there." Mrs Whiting said, pointing towards the 'Death Defyer'.

"Mmm, I know what you mean, it's very fast isn't it?" Mum said. The two of them chatted politely. James watched his little brother. He seemed to be having rather an interesting conversation with Missy.

The two of them were giggling. They seemed to be playing, but as James watched he realised they didn't seem to be playing with each other, but with something else. Something that wasn't there.

James looked at them oddly. It was more than an imaginary friend. In fact he was sure he heard another giggle, a third voice, a high pitched warble.

Indeed, Marmalu was having a very difficult time not laughing. Those two kids kept on pinching him and tickling him. They loved the way his body wobbled like a jelly. Marmalu hoped their Mums wouldn't take too much notice of what their children were actually saying.

"Yook, he all wobbly!" And:

"He got blue skin! And big eyes!" These might have been a bit of a give away!

"James, what's the matter, love?" asked his Mum.

James jumped. He shook his head. He pulled his tissue out of his jacket, and pretended to blow his nose. He could hardly say, "the kids are talking to some weird invisible creature!" He watched them thoughtfully, he would need some evidence before he said anything to anyone.

Sam, Lena and their Dad got off their seats.

"Wow!" Dad wiped his brow, "That was great!" He put his arm around Lena and gave her a squeeze, "Are you OK, you look a bit pale?" Lena nodded,

"I'll be OK!" She gave a weak smile.

"Hi, over here!" Mum was shouting. They walked over to her.

"Look who I bumped into.!" She said. Sam and Lena looked at James with blank faces.

"Hello" They mumbled tonelessly, to be polite. Luckily their Mum seemed to get the hint, she stood up, swinging Missy up on her hip.

"It was nice running into you," she said to James' mum with a smile. "see you later!"

"Bye!" James' mum replied.

"Bye!" said James' little brother and he waved. Sam and Lena waved at him.

"Aw, how does James have such a cute little brother?" Lena said.

"Yeah, but who's he waving at?" Sam hissed.

"What do you mean?"

"Marmalu, he's waving bye to Marmalu!" hissed Sam "come on let's get away from them!"
Sam and Lena ran ahead,

"Marmalu?" Sam whispered.

"Marmalu here! Kids were tickling Marmalu!" he giggled.

"Oh, Marmalu, this is getting very stressful!" Lena said as she jogged along.

"Hey!" Dad shouted "What's the hurry?" He and Mum and Missy caught them up. Sam made some excuse about getting in the queue for the Log Flume. They sighed and climbed the steps to the end of the queue.

"At least we can all go on that one!" said Mum, giving Missy a squeeze. "look, Missy, a ride for you!" Missy giggled and pointed at Marmalu.

"Ride?" she said, meaning was Marmalu going on too. Mum didn't seem to think anything unusual.

"Yes, Sam and Lena and Mummy and Daddy and Missy!" she said, tickling Missy's tummy. Missy smiled. She had seen Sam's face, he had gestured 'shhh!' to her. Missy giggled again.

"Aw, she's so excited, isn't she?" Dad climbed into the log flume ride, and put Missy next to him, Mum squeezed in on the other side, and Sam and Lena sat behind them. Missy looked back at Marmalu, who was squelched in between them, she couldn't stop giggling.

"He must look really funny!" Sam whispered.

"Marmalu bit squooshed!" he warbled quietly. Lena laughed. They set off, up the tracks and under the tunnel.

"Dark, Daddy!" said Missy,

"Yes, sweetie, it's going to go really fast now!"

Everyone cheered as the ride swept down the

water chute and turned the end at the bottom. Missy was having fun. She waved her little chubby hand at the other little kids who all seemed to be looking over at them and pointing. They got off. Lena heard her mum whisper to Dad,

"Have you noticed how people keep pointing at us?" She was starting to get a little paranoid. "Well, kids anyway." She added. Dad just shrugged,

"They're just kids."

Sam noticed that his Mum was getting more and more aware of the stares throughout the day. The theme park was now closing. They made their way to the car park and got into the car. A little girl with her family, was getting into the car next to them. She stared at Marmalu. Mum noticed her looking.
"Hello!" she said to the little girl, "have you had a nice day?" She smiled politely at the girl's mother who smiled back.

"She's loved it! Have you?"
Missy nodded. The other little girl was still staring.

He mouth wide open.

"Jenny, what are you looking at?" her mother asked, not wanting this other family to think her little girl was being rude. Jenny was, of course, gazing at Marmalu.

"Jenny!" The little girl jumped and pointed at Marmalu.

"What is it Mummy?" Her mother was now feeling embarrassed and picked the little girl up and put her in the car. She smiled at their Mum,

"Kids, eh!" They close the car doors and set off, leaving Mum looking a little bewildered.

"There's something weird going on today!" she said sitting in the car. She looked at Sam, who looked mystified and Lena who looked elsewhere and Missy who giggled.

"Kids." Dad shrugged.

They set off for home.

CHAPTER 9

'Espionage'

On Monday morning Sam and Lena had to go to school as usual. After a lot of discussion, they made Marmalu promise to be good and stay invisible, and to listen out for their mum.

"She might want to come in to make the beds or something so be careful!" Lena cave him a squeeze. "See you in a bit."

They left him lying on Sam's bed, watching TV. Marmalu was sad, he didn't like being left alone, but he knew he had to be good.

Mum parked up at school,

"See you later, have a nice day you two!"

"Bye Mum!" They both ran through the big blue doors, it was just gone 9 O clock. To their annoyance, James was at the door. He was monitoring late comers.
"Tut, tut, tut, you're late!" he shook his head and waved his finger at them in a really annoying manner.

"Shut up James, it's only two minutes past.

"You've been late four times this month, so this will make it five. Tell you what, I won't report you if you tell me what's going on with you and that thing you've got staying with you." James put his hands in his pockets and stared at them smugly. Lena looked at Sam in horror, James couldn't know, he couldn't possibly know anything for sure. Sam just shook his head.

"James, you've been sat there too long, the pressure must be getting to you. He pretended to feel James' forehead to check for illness. He laughed.

"I'll find out!" James shouted after them. "You won't get away with it!" He smoothed his hair down where Sam had messed it up and frowned as he saw them whispering up ahead. He pushed his pencil into the notebook furiously. The lead snapped. James growled in annoyance. His friend Judith sidled up to him and the two of them began whispering.

"What are we gonna do, Sam?" Lena asked in panic, Sam shrugged,

"Nothing! Think about it, he knows nothing, he can't see Marmalu, he's invisible, there's nothing to worry about."

He patted her on the shoulder. Lena nodded.

"Mmm, I wish I had your confidence!" She waved

half - heartedly as she headed down the corridor to her classroom.

"I just hope he stays invisible!" Sam muttered to himself as he sat down. Lena didn't see her brother until afternoon break, and she ran up to him.

"I'm really worrying, Sam, what if Marmalu is discovered? Everyone will go mad, it will be like one of those films, you know where everyone turns on the alien, and want to do tests on him. If anyone knows we have a creature from another planet staying with us, Marmalu might be in danger!" She began biting her nails.

Sam tried his best to reassure her, and they walked back into school.

After they'd gone, Judith and James emerged from behind the wall where they'd been standing.

"An alien!" Judith said gleefully.

"Did they say Marmalade?" James frowned.

"Well, did you get it all?" Judith smirked.

"Oh yes!" James sneered, and tapped the tape recorder gently. "I think Mr. Kurtson will want to know about this.

CHAPTER 10

'A disco with a difference'

The next day passed by quickly, Lena was still worried, but Marmalu loved staying in their room, although he was getting a little fed up, he kept begging to come with them to school but Lena said no. Wednesday night was to be the school disco, all the juniors were going, it was a yearly event to raise money for the school fund.

"Wish Marmalu come!" He said sadly as Sam and

Lena got ready, "Marmalu never been dance!"

"Marmalu, I'm sorry but its not safe!" Sam said. "We'd love you to come but it's not safe for you."

"Why not safe?" Marmalu asked , his big eyes wide in wonder, little Yoochoo on his knee, also looking at her soulfully.
Lena sighed, she didn't want to scare him.

"Some people aren't nice, some people wouldn't want you to be here!" She said as nicely as she could manage.

"Marmalu be invisible, no one see, Marmalu safe!"

"He's got a point, Lena, and he's been stuck in for days!" Sam said

"What about Judith and James sticking their big noses in all the time?"

"Well, what about it, they can't prove what they can't see!"

They argued for some time, until Lena reluctantly agreed that it wasn't fair for Marmalu to be stuck in on his own again.

"Goodee!" Marmalu cried, "What Marmalu wear?"
"What will you wear? You will be invisible, it doesn't matter!" Sam laughed. Marmalu looked disappointed, he had his eye on Lena's sparkly dress.

Sam and Lena waved to their mum as she left them by the school's front door, which was wide open for the evening. Marmalu was holding Sam's arm, as instructed. They went in and their hearts sank, James and Judith were in the foyer.
James smiled sweetly.

"Two pounds please!"

Lena handed the money over and they walked past without a word. She could hear whisperings as soon as they moved away.

"I don't trust them!" Lena hissed in Sam's ear.

"Marmalu, you stay away from those two, promise?" Marmalu nodded, which of course they couldn't see.

"Marmalu?"

"Yes?"

"Did you hear me?"

"Yes, stay away from those two!" Marmalu whispered.
Lena smiled, squeezing his hand.
Sam promised to hold on to Marmalu, as Lena went to find her friends.
The school hall was packed, they had a DJ at the far end, with big speakers and flashing disco lights and everything, and all down one side were tables full of crisps, sausage rolls, sandwiches, cheese on sticks, and jugs of lemonade and orange.
Lena was having a great time.
Sam, however spent most of his time on the other side of the hall, which had rows of chairs for the reluctant dancers. He and Marmalu sat down.
Marmalu kept whispering to him,

"What she doing?" As a girl from Lena's class did a spin and landed on the floor.

"Making an idiot of herself!" Sam murmured.

"What that?" As a particularly beaty dance tune came on.

"Its still music, music is all different!" Sam explained.

"Ooh" Marmalu fell silent and just jiggled to the music. To Sam's dismay, James and Judith came and sat right beside him.
James leaned towards him,

"Not got your alien friend with you then?" He asked.
Sam began to panic. Its okay, he told himself, Marmalu is invisible don't worry. He held his hand behind his ear,
"Sorry can't hear you."

"Everyone would love to see him, its not fair to keep him all to yourself!" Judith added, with a fake smile.

"My father would be very interested."

Sam shuddered, he knew for a fact that Judith's father was some sort of scientist.

"I don't know what your taking about!" Sam said, "Your both going crazy!"

He wanted to walk off, but was afraid that Marmalu might say something.
"Pity you feel that way!"

Suddenly James stood up and waved his arms about. To Sam's surprise Mr Kurtson nodded. The music stopped. Into the hall marched a group of men in blue boiler suits armed with what looked like fire extinguishers.

"What's going on?" everyone was complaining as the music stopped. Including the other teachers, who looked furious. Mr. Kurtson signalled to the men, and suddenly the whole room and everyone in it was being covered with foam.
Amidst all the yelling and shouting, Mr Kurtson's voice came through the speakers.

"I do apologise for this, children, but somebody here has brought something into the building which can only be described as, an illegal entity."

Nobody was really listening, they were all too busy wiping foam from their faces. Some were screaming, some were laughing. Most of them thought it was part of the disco experience. Lena looked for Sam urgently.
Sam looked beside him in horror, where was Marmalu? He would be covered in stuff and everyone would see him.
James was also looking for Marmalu, to his immense disappointment, and to Sam's delight, there was no sign of him.
Sam looked over to Lena, who was covered in foam, she came running over. As soon as she saw James, she realised she shouldn't mention Marmalu. Mr Kurtson was still talking.

"There can be no hiding, invisible or not, you will be seen in this room now!" He shouted, waving his fist triumphantly.

"What's he on about?" People were saying.

"He's lost the plot!" A teacher mumbled.

"You better call someone!" Another said, looking worried.

Lena and Sam stood together both wondering where on earth Marmalu had gone to, and how he knew what was going to happen. They were so glad he wasn't in that room right then.

"Where have you hidden him?" Judith was stamping her foot.
"My daddy will be furious! We promised we'd prove the alien was here."

"Mr Kurtson will be furious!" James mumbled as Mr Kurtson was being dragged away from the microphone by Mrs. Stoke.

"Take him to the staff room, Jean, while we wait for them to come!" Mrs Stoke said, and handed the howling Mr. Kurtson over to several teachers.

"There there Mr. Kurtson, let's have a cup of coffee!" Jean soothed him. They obviously thought he'd gone balmy.

"Phew!" Lena sighed. Judith glared at her.

"He was here wasn't he? You helped him get away! Well just you wait, I'll get you!" Judith seethed.

"I don't know what you mean, Judith!"

Mrs Stokes took the microphone

"I am so sorry everyone, that your event has been spoiled by, well, by a very confused individual. However I am sure Mr. Kurtson will soon be better. Your parents have been called, I am afraid we will have to end tonight's disco, and re schedule for another time. I am so sorry!" Poor Mrs Stokes was almost in tears.

 The foam covered children sat down solemnly on the chairs as the teachers ran around with paper towels helping people wipe the worst of it from their clothes.
Sam and Lena didn't dare mention Marmalu whilst in earshot of James or Judith.
As soon as she got the chance Lena grabbed Sam,

"We have to find him, where can he be?"

They searched as best as they could without drawing attention to themselves, but there was no sign of Marmalu.
Soon the parents were arriving,

"Mum and Dad will be here soon, we have to find him!" Lena hissed urgently. They searched in all the class rooms, calling his name in whispered voices, but their was no response. Lena was almost in tears.

 "He'll be scared, we shouldn't have brought him!" Sam looked panicked.
"Lena what if he's gone, gone home? If his parents on Xanlee thought he wasn't safe, they might have zapped him back up there!"

"Sam and Lena!" Mrs Stokes was saying. They jumped and turned to her. "Your parents are here, dears, sorry for the ruined evening!" She said softly, patting Lena gently on the shoulder, obviously assuming that was why she was upset.

They got into the car sadly. Their mum wasn't too pleased with the school for the ruined clothes, and their parents talked about it asking them about the strange actions of Mr. Kurtson all the way home. Missy was belted in her car seat, she looked at them with a puzzled expression. "Marmu?" She asked. Then did the 'all gone!' thing with her hands that mum had taught her. Sam nodded, and Missy went quiet.

"You might as well get changed into your pyjamas, kids - and put your clothes in the wash basket!" Mum said as they came in the house.
They went upstairs slowly and silently.

"I feel terrible , Sam. What can we do? We'll have to go and search for him."

"If he's invisible that's gonna be hard." Sam said sorrowfully. Lena pulled her pyjamas off her bed and plodded towards the bathroom sadly.

"U been ages!" A warble voice said. Lena dropped her pyjamas on the landing and came running back into the bedroom.
There was Marmalu, sat on Sam's bed, as if

nothing had happened.

"Where were you?" Sam shouted, "We were looking for you. Lena was upset!"

"Marmalu hid outside, wait for you to get in car!" He looked confused.

"You can't have been in the car, Missy would have seen you!" Sam said.

"Marmalu hide on floor!"
"Why why did you leave Sam, I told you to stay!" Lena shouted.

"Sorry!" Marmalu pulled a sulky face, "Found this, wanted to see what it was, not want you to take it away, so Marmalu hide!"

In Marmalu's blue hand was a mini tape recorder. Sam and Lena looked at each other.

"Where was it?" Lena asked softly.
Marmalu just shrugged.
"Sorry for shouting. We were worried, we thought we'd lost you!" Lena added.

"On James' seat in the disco!" Marmalu explained.

"James!" Lena snarled.
They pressed the play button, and heard their own voices recorded from a few days earlier.

"So this is what he played to Mr. Kurtson!" Sam seethed.

"Then Mr. Kurtson called in those guys with the stupid foam!" Lena said.

"But his little plot didn't work because Marmalu here had sneaked off to play with this!" Sam said, shaking the tape, "Well, I think we'll keep this bit of evidence, James can't prove the existence of our Marmalu with no tape!"

"Marmalu in trouble?" Marmalu asked looking up with his big round eyes.
Lena shook her head, and gave him a comforting squeeze.

"Definitely not! Well done, Marmalu. It's going to be OK! It looks like we can keep you for a while yet."

Sam gave her a look. She coughed. "I mean, you can stay!"

They both grinned.

CHAPTER 11

Aliens among us.

The local paper which came through the letterbox the next day, had a picture of Mr. Kurtson being put in a car. A tearful Mrs Stokes could be seen in the background, looking on.
'Local teacher loses control' The headline read.

"Loses the plot more like!" Dad had murmured, as he read the paper.
"The guy thought there was an alien in the building, he had it on good authority! That's what it says. Good authority. Ha. As if anyone would

believe there was an alien in the school? What does it do after school I wonder - go and stay with one of its school friends? The man's potty!"

Sam and Lena sat on the sofa with a squashy Marmalu squeezed between them. Missy was babbling away to him, while Lena was trying to tickle Yoochoo who was snuggled in her pocket, but Dad hadn't noticed. He shook his head as if he couldn't believe what he was reading.

"Have you heard this, you two? That Mr. Kurtson thinks one of the kids at your school has got an alien to stay! An alien called Marmalade apparently." He sighed deeply, shaking his head.

Sam and Lena and a very quiet, invisible, Marmalu, laughed.

"Marmalade? No, Dad, we can honestly say we have never met an alien called Marmalade!"

AUTHOR'S NOTE

Thank you for reading this story, I hope you
enjoyed Maramalu's first adventure
here on Earth!

More from
The Xanlean Exchange
coming soon.

Printed in Great Britain
by Amazon.co.uk, Ltd.,
Marston Gate.